PUFFIN BOOKS

# FRYING AS USUAL

Francetti's Fish Restaurant never closes, but this time it looks as if it will – Mr Francetti is lying in hospital with a broken leg, and his wife is visiting her parents in Italy. No one wants to call Mrs Francetti back from her well-earned rest, but how can they manage to keep the chip-shop open? With Grandpa's help, Toni, Rosita and Paula decide they know enough to keep things going, but they hadn't realized before just how difficult frying can be! There are all kinds of problems – the least of which is keeping their extrovert father happy! But in true Francetti style they all rise to a challenge and come up with a few ideas of their own – but will they keep their customers happy?

Joan Lingard is an internationally successful author of books for children and adults. She is also a television playwright. She enjoys travelling and particularly likes France, where she would like to live for a while.

# Frying as Usual

## Joan Lingard

### Illustrated by Kate Rogers

Puffin Books

PUFFIN BOOKS

Published by the Penguin Group
Penguin Books Ltd, 27 Wrights Lane, London W8 5TZ, England
Penguin Books USA Inc., 375 Hudson Street, New York, New York 10014, USA
Penguin Books Australia Ltd, Ringwood, Victoria, Australia
Penguin Books Canada Ltd, 10 Alcorn Avenue, Toronto, Ontario, Canada M4V 3B2
Penguin Books (NZ) Ltd, 182–190 Wairau Road, Auckland 10, New Zealand

Penguin Books Ltd, Registered Offices: Harmondsworth, Middlesex, England

First published in this edition by Hamish Hamilton 1986
Published in Puffin Books 1987
5 7 9 10 8 6

Printed in England by Clays Ltd, St Ives plc
Typeset in Times

# 1. Mr Francetti Falls Off The Roof

"Come quickly," yelled Rosita. "Papa has fallen off the roof."

Toni came at once, letting his book slide to the floor. He ran out of the room after his younger sister. Paula moved more slowly, as was her custom. To begin with, she did not believe it was as urgent as Rosita had suggested. Rosita loved drama and enjoyed nothing more than to be the bearer of bad news. Their father would probably have slipped a few yards. Paula painted her last finger-nail frosted pink and then followed them.

They lived in the flat above their fish and chip shop. She went downstairs, through the closed café, and out into the back yard. There, lying on the ground, his leg twisted in an awkward position, was their father. He was a big, heavily-built man, and he, like Rosita, enjoyed expressing himself fully. He was roaring like a bull and Paula feared that Mrs Small the haberdasher from next door might not care for some of the words he was using.

"Run and phone for an ambulance, Paula," said

Rosita, who knelt at her father's side trying to stroke his brow.

"An ambulance?" said Paula. "Is it that bad?"

"Who can tell?" Toni shrugged. "You know Father."

They had heard him bellow as loudly when he got a splinter in his foot. He had been chopping up wood in the yard in his bare feet at the time. A stupid thing to do, their mother had yelled back at him, and they had quietly agreed though would not have dared to say so. He had hopped around the yard with a splinter of wood sticking out of the sole of his foot for a full five minutes until his wife suggested that he sit down and let her remove it with a darning needle. Rosita had been sent through to buy a brand new one from Mrs Small. But Mrs Francetti was not here now to make such decisions. She had gone to Italy for a month to visit her aged parents who lived in a remote part of Calabria and whom she had not seen for many years. She had sent a glossy card of an olive grove and a bright blue sky.

"My leg's killing me," howled Mr Francetti. "I'm going to die. All alone with Maria far away not even knowing what is happening to me."

"I am here, Papa," said Rosita.

"Better call the doctor," said Toni to Paula. "He'll know whether it's necessary to get an ambulance."

"Get me to hospital. I can't move my leg," Mr

2

Francetti moaned. "I shall die here in the open yard like an animal."

Paula went into the shop and dialled the doctor's surgery. The receptionist said the doctor was out making his calls and was not expected back for at least an hour.

"How serious is it?" she asked.

"I'm not sure," said Paula. "My father says he can't move his leg but then he's inclined to make a bit of a fuss."

"Oh well . . . " The receptionist was beginning to sound bored, as if it was none of her business. "Maybe you'd better try to find out if it is a real emergency. If it is we can get an ambulance. If not, we don't want to waste tax payers' money."

Paula had a vision of an ambulance screaming up the street with its blue light winking, its siren blaring, and neighbours gathered at their doors, and their father getting to his feet saying it mustn't be anything more than a slight strain after all and he'd better get on with the evening's frying. She put down the receiver.

Mr Francetti was still moaning when she returned to the yard.

"Well?" asked Toni.

"The doctor's out on his rounds. And the woman who answered the phone wouldn't have cared if we were all going up in flames."

"Maybe we should call Grandpa?" said Toni.

"Grandpa!" said Paula. "Are you joking? He's probably fast asleep. He must be or he'd have heard the noise."

Grandpa slept a good part of the day though he denied it emphatically. He was also slightly deaf, but not too deaf, and he could hear anything it was to his advantage to hear. This scene in the yard obviously would not be.

"Have you two not done anything yet?" demanded Rosita. "Go and fetch him a drink of water at least."

"Brandy," mouthed Mr Francetti. He moistened his lips. "In the glass cabinet. Behind the china teapot with the roses."

"There you are," said Paula to Rosita. "He can't be that bad."

Toni went to fetch a glass of brandy which Rosita held to her father's lips. He drained the glass quickly.

"A little more," he pleaded. "It helps the pain."

"I don't think alcohol's supposed to be good for shock," said Toni.

"Perhaps sweet tea?" suggested Paula, who had once been a Girl Guide and done a badge on First Aid.

But tea, however sweet, was not what her father felt like at that moment. He appealed to his son. "Be a good boy, Toni, and do what your father tells you.

Another few sips, and I shall be on my feet."

Toni went and Mr Francetti looked at his elder daughter who now knelt beside her sister. "If I do not survive, Paula, you will take the place of your mother until she returns from Calabria. I count on you."

"Don't be silly, Dad. Of course you're going to survive."

"You are hard, my child. You have no idea of the pain I am enduring." He groaned again and Paula noticed there were beads of sweat on his brow. And his face was tinged with grey. For the first time she felt uneasy and wondered if he might really be in pain.

"What were you doing up on the roof?" she asked.

"Replacing some slates that came off in the gale last night. I thought I cannot allow the rain to drip on my poor darlings' heads . . . "

"Poor Papa," murmured Rosita. "You always think of us."

"So, how far did you fall?" asked Paula.

"From the top. Right beside the chimney."

Paula and Rosita looked up. It looked a long way to fall, if he really had come down from the height of the chimney. There was no sign of a ladder, only the steps they used for decorating.

"Did you use a ladder?" asked Paula.

"A ladder? No, no, I stood on the steps and pulled myself up from there. The slates were wet from the

6

rain last night . . . . Oooh, oooh . . . Ah, thank you, Toni."

He raised himself on an elbow and drank from the glass unassisted. Then he sank back again against Rosita's shoulder.

"It was very brave of you to go up there at all," said Rosita.

Especially with his weight, thought Toni.

"You should have asked Toni to do it for you," said Rosita.

"He was busy with his studying," said Mr Francetti. "And that comes first. I will not let my children spend their lives frying fish and chips. You will not be like your old father slicing up potatoes night after night, turning them over and over in hot fat. You will be able to sit in a nice office. If only I had had your chances!"

They did not say anything. They knew he enjoyed frying fish and chips and the bustle of the shop, and that a week sitting behind a desk in an office would have sent him running for mercy up the street to the nearest fish and chip shop. His father had fried fish and chips before him. It was in his blood. It was not in theirs though, strangely enough. They did not mind helping, at least Rosita and Toni did not – Paula hated the smell the frying left on her hair and clothes and was forever washing both – but none of them wanted to spend their lives in the shop.

"So you slipped *right* from the top, Dad?" said Paula.

"Well . . . not quite. It was while I was trying to come down. I could not get my feet to reach the top of the steps."

They could imagine him dangling there, clinging madly to the wet roof, his fingers slipping, his feet ranging around seeking the top step. And then falling. That was how he must have injured his leg.

"I fell with my leg under me," said Mr Francetti.

"Let's see if we can straighten it," said Paula.

"Be careful." Mr Francetti groaned again.

Rosita held his hand whilst Paula and Toni tried gently to lift it. He screamed.

"I think there is something really wrong." Toni looked at Paula.

"Mrs Small goes to the Red Cross," said Rosita. "Maybe she would know what to do."

"Why didn't you say so before?" said Paula crossly. "Here we've been sitting around wasting all this time with an expert on our doorstep."

Rosita shinned over the back wall and dropped down into Mrs Small's yard. She opened her back door, went through the little sitting-room behind the shop where Mrs Small drank sly cups of tea and stored her bundles of wool and boxes of elastic and thread. The little lady, so deserving of her name, was behind

8

the counter showing zip fasteners to a customer.

"Mrs Small, my father's fallen off the roof," said Rosita. "Please come at once."

Mr Small dropped the collection of zips. "Oh, my goodness! What a fright you gave me, child!"

"Papa's given us a fright too. He could be dying."

"Oh dear me, surely not." Mrs Small regarded Rosita with her mild blue eyes. She also had experience of Rosita's dramatic announcements. "One moment till I finish serving this lady and then I'll come." She had promised Mrs Francetti before her departure that she would keep an eye on her brood.

The customer took away her zip and then Mrs Small went next door with Rosita, going by the front since she was not young or nimble enough for scaling back walls. Her eyes grew more anxious when she saw the colour of Mr Francetti's face.

"We've been trying to straighten his leg but we can't seem to do it," said Paula.

"That's the very worst thing you could do. You must always leave injuries to those who are able to handle them. Toni, go at once and phone for an ambulance."

Toni went.

"I kept telling them," said Mr Francetti. "But they wouldn't listen. They thought I was just fussing."

"There now, just lie quiet. Rosita, dear, go and

mind the shop for me in case I have a customer."

Rosita looked back at her father. Normally she enjoyed looking after Mrs Small's shop, on the odd occasions that she was permitted to. She liked the balls of wool and trays of thread of every colour of the rainbow.

"It's all right. I'll look after him," promised Mrs Small. "And you'll see the ambulance when it arrives."

Mr Francetti renewed his groaning as if he thought it necessary to justify the calling of the ambulance.

"It's all right, Mr Francetti," said Mrs Small. "Try not to excite yourself."

"Impossible," muttered Paula.

Rosita settled herself behind Mrs Small's counter, having first of all put away the unwanted zips. When the door opened she looked up to see her friend Susan entering. Susan had come for a card of elastic for her mother. Rosita served her with a flourish and told the tale of her father's fall, giving full details of everything that had happened, and perhaps of a few that had not. Embroidering: that was what her mother would have called it.

"Something's always happening to your father," said Susan.

As Rosita sellotaped the little parcel, using more sellotape than Mrs Small would have approved of, they heard the wail of the ambulance in the street. They rushed to the door.

Soon the street was full of people: neighbours, passers-by, customers from the surrounding shops. A few minutes later Mr Francetti was carried out on a stretcher covered with a red blanket. Rosita ran forward.

"Will you be all right, Papa?" she asked.

"Don't worry, darling," said her father, lifting his head. "I am being looked after now."

"Somebody will have to accompany him," said the driver of the ambulance. "To bring back his clothes if they keep him in."

"I want Paula to come," Mr Francetti moaned from inside the ambulance. "She must take her mother's place."

Paula swallowed. She hated hospitals. Even the smell in the corridors made her feel sick. But she climbed into the back of the ambulance, and the driver shut the door.

"You mustn't worry, Rosita," said Mrs Small as they watched it drive away. "It may be something quite simple. Like a strain. He might be back tonight."

Rosita blew her nose and smiled bleakly. She knew that Mrs Small was just trying to comfort her.

"I'll see you later, Rosita," said Susan. Her mother

would be wondering where she had got to with the elastic.

The crowd dispersed now that there was nothing else to see. Rosita and Toni looked round and saw that Grandpa was standing in the doorway of the shop in his carpet slippers. His grey bushy hair was tousled.

"What's going on?" he asked.

"Papa fell off the roof," said Rosita.

"The roof?"

"Yes," said Toni. "He's gone to hospital."

"Hospital?"

"In an ambulance."

"But what for? He fell off the roof before."

It was true: their father had slipped when he had been fixing the television aerial on the chimney, but that had been a few years ago and they had forgotten. He was so accident-prone that they could not remember all his disasters.

"So what's he gone for this time?"

"To get X-rays and things," said Toni. "He's hurt his leg."

"Ah, he likes a fuss!" The old man tossed his head. "Always the same ever since a baby. He bumps his head on his mother's chin and you'd think he had fallen down the stairs."

"This time I think it may be a little more serious, Mr Francetti," said Mrs Small. "Your son's leg was lying at a very odd angle." She left them to go back into her own shop where a customer was waiting for her.

Grandpa took out his pocket watch and held it close to his eyes. "Do you know the hour?"

"No," said Rosita, still thinking of the ambulance taking her father through the streets to the hospital.

"Five!"

"Five," repeated Rosita.

"The shop should be open," said Toni.

"Exactly," said the old man. "And here we stand on the pavement with the frying not begun."

"But can we do it?" said Toni. He did not even know what temperature the oil should be.

"Can we do it?" Grandpa was indignant. He smoothed out his moustache. "For forty years I fried nightly."

But that was more than ten years ago, thought Toni, when you could see and hear properly and your hands didn't shake. If only their mother were here . . .

"Let us go in," said Grandpa, "and attend to our business. We must fry tonight, like every night."

## 2. Frying Tonight

FRANCETTI'S FISH RESTAURANT.

Above the doorway, the sign was written in large bold red and green letters on a white background. The Italian colours. The colours of their homeland, Mr Francetti had informed passers-by as he stood on the pavement calling up instructions to the sign-painter. He had had the sign repainted in the spring. He had had many instructions to call up to the painter and was lucky that only the odd spot of red or green paint had landed on him.

The front of the shop was plastered with signs of many kinds, some neatly printed, some hastily written, some painted in rainbow colours. Some were on boards, or made of metal; others were stuck to the glass. TEA. COFFEE. FISH SUPPERS. COCA-COLA. CARRY-OUT. FRESH FISH GUARAN-TEED. Advertisements for chocolate bars. At night some of the signs were lit with neon lights. Mr Francetti gave a great deal of thought to the decoration of his shop window.

Inside the door, to the right, stood the big glass

showcase in which bars of chocolate were displayed. The glass sloped backwards and on top of it were ranged bottles of brightly coloured sweets. At the end of the case was the counter where Rosita now waited for customers. Behind her, on the shelves, were more bottles of sweets and packets of cigarettes and matches. She like leaning on the counter taking in the scene. Later on it would get busy, the juke-box would play and the atmosphere would be lively. At the moment it was quiet, which was just as well as the chips weren't ready. People hated waiting for their chips. They'd chink their money against the counter, shift from foot to foot, sigh. Only one man sat at a table to the left of the door. He was drinking a cup of tea which she had made for him and eating a chocolate biscuit. He got up and put a coin into the juke-box. The record began to play. Rosita hummed to the tune.

At the back of the shop was the most important part: the chip counter with the frying vats behind.

"A man never forgets his trade," declared Grandpa. "Even when he is denied the right to practise it." His son always kept him out of the cooking area, a bitter point of resentment. Grandpa had given up arguing years ago.

"I suppose not," murmured Toni unbelievingly, as he peered into the sizzling vat of oil and potatoes. The first lot they had had to throw away as the oil had been

too cold and the chips had turned out pale and soggy. "No one will notice," Grandpa had said, but to Toni they had looked revolting so he had insisted on discarding them. He thought the old man had not been able to see them clearly enough. Now Toni wondered if the oil was not too hot. The potatoes were browning rapidly, very rapidly, before they could possibly be cooked in the middle. And there was a smell of burning. Toni said so.

"Burning, boy? You imagine it."

"I don't think so. Rosita, come here a moment!"

Rosita came, waving her hand in front of her eyes to ward off the smoke.

"Do you smell burning?" asked Toni.

"I certainly do!" Rosita began to cough and splutter.

Another lot for the dustbin. And all the doors had to be left open to allow the smoke to get out. The wind swirled in from the street bringing in the autumn leaves.

They set to work again peeling another batch of potatoes, putting them into the slicing machine and carrying them through to the vats in buckets.

"We must approach this business of temperature in a much more scientific frame of mind," said Toni.

"What kind of mind is that?" asked Grandpa suspiciously.

17

"We are going to test the temperature of the oil with a thermometer."

"That is not the way." Grandpa shook his head. "Temperature is something that one *knows*. In the way that a pianist knows if he plays the right note on the piano. You never see your papa with a thermometer."

"Maybe not. But he's not here."

"I never in my life used a thermometer either." The old man spoke as if it were a slur on his honour. He was not happy when Toni went upstairs and reappeared with the instrument. He wiped his hands down the white coat that belonged to his son. The coat hung loosely on his body and swirled around his ankles. His son was a fine big man and he could not see why he had had to go away in an ambulance and lie in a hospital bed just because he had done a little thing like slip off a roof. Especially when they had been just about to start frying.

Three girls came in. They were in the class above Rosita at school.

"Three fish suppers!" said the one in the middle, laying a five pound note on the counter. The note looked crisp and new. The girl smoothed it out so that her two friends could admire it.

"I'm sorry," said Toni, "but we're not quite ready yet."

"Our father had an accident," put in Rosita. "He fell off the roof."

"Fell off the roof?" One of the girls began to laugh and then the other two started up.

"It's no laughing matter," said Rosita indignantly.

But the girls seemed to think that it was. The one with the money recovered first.

"How long till you will be ready?" she asked.

"Ten, fifteen minutes," said Toni.

"Fifteen minutes! I'm starving."

"There's plenty other chip shops, Mandy," said one of her friends.

"There's 'Sea Breezes' round the corner," said the other. "It's great. Everybody's going there now."

'Sea breezes' had opened only a month ago. It was brightly painted and glittered with chromium fittings and it had taken away quite a bit of the Francettis' custom. Mr Francetti had been heard to declare that he wished a gigantic breeze would blow the place out into the middle of the Atlantic Ocean. It was one of a chain of chip shops and not run by a family, as theirs was.

"Yeah, let's go," said Mandy. "I'm not hanging about here waiting." She lifted up her crisp five pound note. Rosita watched her push it into the pocket of her jeans.

The three girls put their backs to the counter and moved towards the door.

"Some dump this is." Mandy looked round at the walls which Mr Francetti intended to redecorate when he could afford it.

"Fancy falling off the roof!"

They were overcome with laughter again. The door swung to behind them.

"Ha, ha," said Rosita. "Very funny."

"You see, Toni, now we lose custom!" Grandpa threw up his hands.

"Who'd want their custom?" Rosita muttered. She'd never liked that Mandy girl. A real show-off she was. Her father owned a recording studio, or so she said. Probably taped records in his back shed.

"It's not my fault," said Toni, lowering the thermometer into the oil.

"You should have kept the first batch. There was nothing wrong with them." As Grandpa waved his hand he knocked Toni's arm. Toni lost the thermometer in the vat of swirling oil.

"Now look!" said Toni.

"Ah, throw in the potatoes!" Grandpa threw in a handful. They sizzled in what seemed to Toni to be the right manner. He emptied in the rest.

Rosita filled up the salt and pepper pots, and the sauce and vinegar bottles. She wiped all the rims of the bottles as her mother did, for her mother hated messy bottle tops where the sauce coagulated and bulged beneath the rim of the top. You could always tell a good fish restaurateur by the state of his bottles, said her mother. Rosita gave each table an extra polish so that the red formica shone.

"Shall I put on the lights?" she asked Toni.

"Yes. It's almost dark."

She liked the shop best when the lights were on. The colours were brighter, the bottles of sweets shone. She liked evening. She was a night-bird, her mother said.

The smell began to fill the shop. Rosita sniffed. It was the right smell now, no trace of scorching. She suddenly realised she was hungry. They had not eaten since lunch-time.

"I'm starved," she said.

"I too," confessed Grandpa. "Perhaps we may have a little supper ourselves."

Toni wiped his forehead with the back of his sleeve. His face was flushed bright red and his dark hair plastered close to his head. It had been a heavy hour. And there would be loads and loads more chips to make tonight, with chicken and fish to fry and pies to heat . . . And he had maths homework to do for the morning. He hoped Paula wouldn't dilly-dally on the way home. He knew her, how she could take an hour to cover one block. She had a knack of meeting school friends and standing talking and then coming in to say she had forgotten what time it was. He wanted, too, to hear about his father.

They ate a plate of fish and chips each, sitting at one of the tables. Toni got up twice to serve customers during his meal. He would not let Rosita do it even though she was more than willing. He said she was too young, she might burn herself.

"He is a very serious young man," said Grandpa when Toni went to serve one customer.

"He doesn't let me get away with much," said Rosita.

"He has to stand in his father's place."

And Paula was supposed to stand in her mother's. She would have a job doing that.

Toni came back to the table. "I hope Dad's only got a sprain. A break would take ages to mend."

"He has sprained every part of his body in his time," said Grandpa.

"How does he manage it?" asked Rosita.

"He takes foolish risks."

She smiled. She did not mind that.

"Toni here will not take risks," said Grandpa. "He will go with a thermometer in his hands."

"It wastes less time," said Toni. "And money. Ah, here comes Paula, thank goodness!"

They turned to see Paula coming in.

"How is Papa?" asked Rosita at once.

22

"He isn't going to die," said Paula.

"We didn't think he would," said Toni.

"But he's broken his leg."

"Broken?" repeated Toni.

"Compound fracture, above the thigh," said Paula.

"Doesn't sound too good," said Toni.

"Take very long time to mend," said Grandpa. "What an idiot Giorgio is! It is just like him to go and do this thing when Maria is in Italy."

"They said he would probably be in hospital for at least a fortnight," said Paula. "And after that he would have to go to a convalescent home unless there was someone here to look after him."

"There isn't," said Toni. "He's going to love that, weeks in hospital and convalescent homes! Can you imagine his temper?"

"I wouldn't like to be one of the nurses," said Paula.

"So what are we going to do?" asked Rosita, looking round at them all. "It doesn't mean we'll have to close the shop, does it?"

"Close the shop?" Grandpa rose to his feet. "We Francettis have never closed. We shall carry on together."

"Hurrah!" shouted Rosita.

"I suppose we can do it," said Toni. "But we'll all have to work jolly hard. You too, Paula."

Paula sniffed the air. "Isn't there something burning?"

"It's the fish!" cried Toni, and dashed behind the counter.

## 3. Francetti's Never Closes

People were streaming towards the hospital carrying bunches of flowers and bags of fruit and plastic boxes full of tempting titbits. Rosita carried three cakes she had made from melted chocolate and cornflakes in a little round tin. On the bus she'd kept easing up the lid of the tin and breaking off tiny pieces of chocolate and now she saw that the cakes looked considerably smaller than they had been when she set out. She had wanted to buy her father some golden chrysanthemums with big curly heads but Paula had told her not to be ridiculous. Their father was not a flowery man.

They went down the drive and into the corridors of the hospital. Rosita liked the smells and the chink of instruments. There was promise of great drama behind all those closed doors. They found the ward easily and their father's bed too for they heard his voice before they saw him. He was roaring at a nurse who had accidentally touched the end of his bed.

His broken leg was suspended high in a pulley and swathed in plaster.

"Completely immobilised," murmured Toni. "I never thought I'd see the day."

"Well, my poor chickens," their father greeted them, "and how are you all doing without your old father to look after you?"

"We're managing fine," said Toni.

"Come kiss me then, all of you."

They kissed him and Rosita presented her offering.

"What have we here?" cried her father, jerking open the lid of the tin and peering inside. Rosita, taking an anxious look, saw that the cakes looked somewhat jumbled as if they had been thrown up in the air and caught again. Her father lifted out a chocolate-coated cornflake and laid it on his tongue. "Delicious," he pronounced. He patted the edge of the bed. "You may sit beside me, child, but you must be careful not to move an inch. It is agony, agony, if someone bangs against me! You see that stupid nurse over there? She is so clumsy, so clumsy!"

The nurse approached and said, "I'm sorry, you're only allowed two visitors at a time."

"Two visitors at a time! What nonsense is this?"

"It is a hospital regulation," said the nurse.

"Regulations! I pay no attention to them."

"It's for your own good, Mr Francetti, so that you won't get too tired out."

"Tired out! You do not know me. Every night I

26

serve hundreds with fish and chips in my restaurant and at the end of the day I could run round the park three times."

"But not with a broken leg."

"Run away, little girl." He waved his hand at her and she went, giving him a sharp look over her shoulder.

"Now then, give me all the news." After they had told him what was suitable for him to know, their father said, "So it seems that you can manage." He did not sound convinced. "I was wondering if I should cable to Calabria and recall your mother. We have been having a hard time in the shop recently. It is those other two shops that are doing it to us. 'Sea Breezes' – " he snorted " – what a name! And the 'Golden Fish'. They serve plastic fish. But people are too stupid to notice. Perhaps I should call your Mother home."

"No, don't," said Paula. "Please, Father. She hasn't had a holiday since she got married. She told me so before she went. It's not fair."

"It's not my fault," replied her father. "We have to work hard and make money so that we can keep you children at school. We cannot shut the shop, we cannot leave it in the hands of the old man. He is too far gone in his dotage to manage such a business now."

"It's all right, Dad," said Toni soothingly. "You don't have to recall Mother, and we can run the shop."

"If you can't then I shall have to send for her. I would not allow the shop to be closed. Those other shops would clean up all our business."

Most of the patients in the ward and their visitors were listening to the conversation. It seemed to be more interesting than anything they had to talk about themselves, and besides, Mr Francetti had what was known as a 'carrying' voice.

"I have made out a notice," he said. "Rosita, look in the locker and you will see it." He smiled and for a moment forgot his pain and discomfort. Making out notices always made him happy. He and his friend Mr Pindi the Indian grocer next door were addicts, and often their windows were covered with so many pieces of paper that one could not see what was offered for sale beyond. When Toni had pointed this out to his father, Mr Francetti had said that then people would be tempted to come inside and find out. Curiosity was a great thing when it came to advertising.

Rosita brought out the notice. It had been printed in two shades of felt tip pen, purple and pink, the colours alternating with each word. It read: "CLOSED AT LUNCH TIME OWING TO UNFORTUNATE AND UNFORESEEN ACCIDENT TO THE

29

PROPRIETOR BUT FRYING AS USUAL EVERY EVENING. FRANCETTI'S NEVER CLOSES." It was signed in green with a flourish: Giorgio Francetti.

Toni and Paula looked at one another over the top of their father's head. They would have to put it up. If not, Mr Pindi would be sure to tell him.

"What a lovely notice!" said Rosita.

"You have inherited my artistic temperament, Rosita," said her father. "You are the only one."

Rosita beamed at him. Poor Papa, she thought, with all those business worries. There must be something she could do to help him. There must be some way she could give the business a boost. She would have to think of a plan . . .

Tony took the paper and promised to sellotape it to the window. They had already put up a simple message saying: "CLOSED AT LUNCH TIME UNTIL FURTHER NOTICE" but there was no point in telling him that.

"Look!" said Rosita. "Here comes Grandpa and Mr Pindi."

Mr Pindi and Grandpa advanced up the ward bringing a delicious blend of smells with them, curry and chips. Mr Pindi carried a bowl covered with a cloth and Grandpa a newspaper package.

"Oh, my dear friends, how kind you are!" Mr Francetti clapped his hands. "You know my favourites.

How I have been longing for some real food! Here they serve me slops fit only for babes in arms and old women."

He took the newspaper parcel and unwrapped it. The chips inside had been liberally doused with salt and sauce and vinegar. "Nectar! Delicious, Papa!"

"I have not lost my touch."

Toni suspected that Grandpa had bought the chips at a café near the hospital.

"And the curry, Mohammet, it is superb." Mr Francetti took a chip, then a dip of curried vegetables. The children's mouths watered as they watched and the smell was enough to make Rosita feel about to swoon. The man in the next bed nearly fell out trying to get a better look.

The nurse came back. Her chin was tilted upwards. "I'm afraid you are not allowed to eat at this time of day, Mr Francetti. You will be having tea after visiting."

"Tea!" he snorted. "Two pieces of brown bread and red glue they call jam. Tea for bambinos!"

The nurse reached out her hand to take the bowl of curry.

"Oh no, you don't." Mr Francetti swung the bowl out of her reach.

"You are supposed to hand in all food to Sister. And you are not allowed *five* visitors!"

31

"Go and find someone who has no visitor and tell him a bedside story."

The nurse went off and they laughed. Everyone else in the ward laughed as well.

"I amuse them, do I not?" said Mr Francetti and dug into his curry.

A few minutes later, the nurse returned. She brought the Sister with her.

"Trouble?" asked Mr Pindi.

"Nothing I can't handle," said Mr Francetti.

His visitors cleared a passage for the Sister. She held herself very straight and clasped her hands in front of her starched apron.

"Mr Francetti," she began.

"Sister," he broke in, "how charming you look today! You have the most beautiful eyes I have ever seen in a woman."

"Now Mr Francetti, don't be ridiculous." Her cheeks were darkening to a delicate shade of rose. Paula was threatening to laugh. Toni warned her with a shake of the head. In fact, his father was right: the Sister did have lovely eyes.

"They are beautiful when you let them soften."

"Mr Francetti – "

"Call me Giorgio."

She said with determination, but not very sternly, "You know that you should not be eating curry and

32

chips at this time of the afternoon."

"Would you like a chip?" Mr Francetti held out the package. "From my own restaurant. They are a bit cold now but still not bad. Tomorrow my father will bring some especially for you. And a piece of fresh fish crisply fried – "

"No thank you, really . . . " She paused. They saw that she was going to give in. She went on less strongly, "And you should not have five visitors all at once but since the visiting hour is nearly ended I will not ask them to go today."

"Sister, you are a delightful woman!"

The Sister clicked away down the ward followed by the nurse who looked back with a baleful glance.

"That young one is a pain," said Mr Francetti. "A kill-joy. But the Sister, she is all right."

"Giorgio," said Grandpa, "Say what you like, but Italian men know how to speak pretty to a woman." He smoothed his moustache proudly.

The bell rang to mark the end of the visiting hour. Mr Francetti finished the curry and wrapped the bowl in the newspaper.

"Thank you, Mohammet, it was good of you to remember me. I shall do the same for you one day. You will come again? And you, my children, you will come daily to report on the state of the business. And

33

remember our slogan: FRANCETTI'S NEVER CLOSES."

"You'd think it was wartime," muttered Paula. She was studying the Second World War in history at school.

"It is in a way," said Rosita. "We're in a state of emergency."

They kissed their father good-bye. They were last to leave the ward. The Sister was standing outside the door.

"I hope our father is making progress," said Toni, feeling that he ought to make some remark.

"He is not the easiest of patients," said the Sister.

"He is not the easiest of fathers," said Paula.

## 4. A Challenge

"It's a challenge," said Toni. "But I'm sure we can do it."

"There speaks a true Francetti," said Grandpa, clapping him on the shoulder.

"It is all a matter of organisation," said Toni, who was making out a list of jobs.

"That sounds less like a Francetti. Your father has never organised himself in his life."

"And look where it's got him!" Paula threw another peeled potato into the bucket and wiping her hands down her apron, straightened her back. She wondered how her mother has stood up to so many years of potato-peeling.

"Rosita, will you take charge of the sweet counter?" said Toni.

Rosita went happily to stand behind the counter. She hummed as she weighed the sweets and rang up the money in the till. She was sorry her father had fallen off the roof but it did have its compensations. In normal times her mother and father ran the fish and chip side of the business between them and Toni and

Paula helped out behind the sweet and cigarette counter when they were busy.

A crowd of boys came in. There were six of them, Rosita counted as they filed past. She didn't like the look of them. They were the kind that made trouble. Their father was good at handling such boys. A roar and a threat from him usually worked. He had a black belt at judo and could throw someone across the floor with the flick of a wrist.

One of the boys put some money in the juke-box. The rest sat at the tables, sprawling their legs across the floor so that it would be difficult for people to pass by.

"Service!" demanded the biggest and toughest looking one and banged the tomato sauce bottle on the table.

"It's self-service here," said Rosita.

He turned to look at her. "Get a load of that! It's self-service is it?" He mimicked her voice. "Can you see over the top of the counter, Tich?" His friends laughed and Rosita thought they were easily amused. She edged an old sweet box along the floor with her feet and stood up on it.

"Grown all of a sudden have you? Somebody watered your feet?"

"It's a pity you can't grow some decent manners," said Rosita.

36

He got up. He came sauntering over to the counter and leant against it. "You've got a big gob on you. Maybe too big."

Toni came quickly round behind Rosita. He eyed the boy. "Can I help you?" he asked.

"We want six spring roll suppers."

"If you'd like to take your place in the queue then you can have them."

"We don't queue for nothing."

"Then you get nothing," said Rosita. She knew Toni would give her a row later. He said it was better to play it cool but she felt anything but cool. She would have liked to have taken the boy by his spiky fair hair and pulled it hard with both hands.

The boy stared at her across the counter. She stared back without blinking although inside herself she could feel her heart going bumpety-bump.

"Rosita, it's time you went to bed," said Toni quietly.

Rosita could have killed him then. As she said to Susan the next day in the playground, you can always rely on brothers to lower your dignity at the wrong moment. Susan was fortunate in that she had no brothers, though Susan did not seem to think so.

"Beddy-byes time," said the boy, laughing softly. "Away you go and get cuddled up with your teddy bear."

Rosita did not move. And she did not look round at her brother.

Now Grandpa came out from behind the counter.

"Trouble?" he asked, wiping his hands, smoothing out his moustaches, pulling back his shoulders.

"No," said Toni. "Everything's fine."

"You can have some trouble if you want it," said the boy.

"We don't, thank you," said Toni. "We've got other things to do." He never roared like his father, but he could also toss someone across the floor if he had to. His father had seen to it that he could.

"I soon fix," said Grandpa, moving forward.

"Is that right, Grandpa?" The youth now turned his attention to the old man.

"That's right. Outa the shop, come on, pronto!"

Toni sighed. His family was marvellous at making trouble where none existed, and when it did, building it from a bubble into a balloon.

The boy's friends were on their feet. They were a troublesome bunch, well-known in the district. They were always hanging round the streets making a noise, kicking things.

"There are plenty other chippers. We don't have to spend our money in this joint."

"We don't want your stinking money anyway," said Rosita.

38

Toni kicked her in the shins.

"You're not going to get it either." The boy turned to face his friends. "Come on, let's blow. This place is a drag."

They ambled towards the door.

"Like sheep," said Rosita loudly. "Follow my leader."

"Rosita!" said Toni warningly.

On the way out one of the boys knocked against a table. He put on a mock display of staggering and hit the table with his other side. The sauce and vinegar bottles slid to the end and went clattering down to the ground. There was the sound of cracking glass and then tomato sauce and vinegar began to ooze out across the floor.

"Tut, tut," said the leader of the gang. The rest doubled up as if they had pains in their stomachs.

Paula came through from the back shop. "What's going on here?" She looked down at the floor and then at the boys.

"Been an accident," said the leader. "Billy cut himself. See his blood. Nice colour isn't it? Cheers!"

"You can set to and clean it up," said Paula.

"You'll be lucky!"

The boys swarmed out on to the pavement.

"Don't bother showing your noses in here again," Rosita called after them.

39

"Rosita, will you never learn to keep your mouth closed?" groaned Toni.

The leader stopped to look round. "Oh, we'll be back all right. Don't worry about that."

And then they were gone.

"I do not like them." Grandpa shook his head.

"Grandpa is marvellous at understatements," said Paula.

"And you are marvellous at being sarcastic," said Rosita.

"There are times when I wish you would all keep your mouths shut," said Toni, going to pick up the broken glass. "You're a great lot for opening them up and getting us into trouble."

"Trouble." Grandpa nodded his head. "That is what they want. They come back for it."

"The leader's called Dan McGill," said Paula. "It's a pity he has to act the tough. He's not bad-looking."

"Paula!" Rosita was outraged. Sisters were a problem too. To declare that the enemy wasn't bad-looking was like an act of treachery.

"He's not got much of a life at home," said Paula. "There's about half a dozen kids and his father's in and out of prison. Mum says his mother's a decent wee woman who does her best. Can't be much fun for him."

"Never mind about that now. This is not much fun

trying to clear up this mess. Go and get a cloth," said Toni, becoming irritable, which he seldom did. But tonight his sisters were not exactly what he would have liked them to be. Standing in the middle of a mess of broken glass and tomato sauce arguing about Dan McGill!

As he lifted the pieces of glass, one jabbed the palm of his right hand. His blood mingled with the ketchup.

"Honestly," said Rosita. "Men!"

"You're getting as bad as Father," said Paula, taking hold of his wrist.

"Thanks for the sympathy." Toni pressed hard on the hand to stifle the pain.

"Let's get it under the tap," said Paula, "and see how bad it is. With all that tomato sauce it's difficult to tell."

"Grandpa, watch the chips," called Toni, as he allowed Paula to lead him through to the kitchen.

When Paula had rinsed off the sauce they saw that the gash was quite deep.

"Might need to be stitched," said Paula.

Toni nodded. "I guess I'd better go along the road to the doctor's." He went out with his hand wrapped in a tea towel.

In the shop the queue at the chip counter had lengthened. Sweat stood out in beads from Grandpa's brow as he scooped up the chips, dressed them and

wrapped them. In his efforts to hurry he dropped chips on the floor, sprinkled salt on the counter and slopped vinegar in every direction.

Rosita came out from behind her counter to join him. "Can I help, Grandpa? I'll be careful."

"Why not? As you say, this is an emergency state."

Toni returned later with his hand wrapped in a snowy white bandage.

"Six stitches," he said gloomily. "I've to go back in ten days to get them out."

"Poor Toni," cried Rosita.

"You won't be able to fry," said Paula, pushing her damp hair back from her forehead. She had been working without stopping all evening, as had Grandpa and Rosita. "How shall we manage now?" she asked.

"You and I and Rosita," said Grandpa. "We manage, we three."

"Of course we manage," said Rosita.

Toni sighed. "There seems to be some kind of jinx on this family at the moment. We could do with a spot of good luck for a change."

"Maybe we'll get it," said Rosita mysteriously. "You never know. I have a feeling we will."

She had been reading a book in the library on how to run a small business. The thing was to promote it. You shouldn't just sit there and wait for things to happen. You had to make them happen. You had to bring the customers in. She had several ideas in her head for doing just that. A plan was beginning to take shape.

"Time you were in bed, Rosita," said Toni, interrupting her thoughts. "Your eyes are looking glazed."

She gave him a small, pitying smile before she went. He would not be sending her up to bed early when she had brought the family business back from the brink of bankruptcy.

## 5. Rosita's Plan

Rosita and Susan crouched at the back of one of the sheds in the school playground eating a bag of salt and vinegar crisps brought by Rosita from the shop. Whenever her father saw her going out to school in the mornings laden with bags of crisps and bars of chocolate for her friends he roared at her. He said that it was no wonder they didn't make a profit, but he had never stopped her taking them.

It was pouring with rain outside so the sheds were full of children eating, talking, or swapping scraps. Scraps were the rage at the moment. Last term it had been 'elastics'. Dozens of elastic bands were strung together, held down by the children's feet to form a triangle, and then you hopped over them in a scissoring movement. The local newsagent had been hard put to keep up with the demand for elastic bands. Now he was left with packets of them collecting dust on his shelves.

Rosita and Susan did not swap scraps: they had too much to talk about. Susan liked to hear of the doings of the Francettis. They were always up to something.

It wasn't half as exciting in her house. She was an only child and her father was an insurance agent. He never fell off roofs and her mother never went away for a day, let alone for a month.

"Susan," said Rosita solemnly. "The Francettis are on the verge of bankruptcy."

"Bankruptcy," said Susan, realising from Rosita's tone that it must be something awesome.

"Our business is in a bad state. Very bad." Rosita shook her head.

"You mean you might have to close the shop?" said Susan, horrified.

"It could come to that." Rosita took out the last two crisps and gave one to Susan. Then she brightened. "But all is not yet lost," she added, lowering her voice. "I have a plan. And I want you to help me, Susie."

"What kind of plan?"

"I'm going to mount a big advertising campaign. I was reading an article the other day and it said advertising was everything. Just think, Susie, when you see chocolate bars advertised on the telly you want to rush out and buy them, don't you?"

"You're not going to advertise your shop on the telly?" said Susan.

"Of course not." Rosita was scornful. She wondered how she put up with Susan at times. You had to spell everything out carefully to her. "There are other ways of advertising. It's a matter of presenting your product in the most attractive fashion."

"But what can you do about fish and chips?" asked Susan.

"You'd be surprised," said Rosita.

The bell rang to mark the end of break. The children gathered up their scraps hastily and sped through the rain to line up. Rosita and Susan rose and strolled after them to join their class.

Business was slack that evening. It often was midweek, Toni reminded them, so it was nothing to worry about. Grandpa would not be convinced.

"We're on the run down," he said. "I never thought I would see the day."

"Don't be daft, Grandpa," said Paula. "It's a wet night. They probably can't be bothered coming out."

"We are down this week on our takings, are we not, Toni?" demanded Grandpa.

"Yes," admitted Toni. "It can't be helped."

"Maybe it can," said Rosita. "If we do extra well at the week-end we might be able to make up for it."

"And how are we to do extra well?" asked Paula. "You can hardly yank people in off the street at gun point."

"You never know," said Rosita. "There are ways and means."

47

"Honestly, Rosita, you're just about as fanciful as Father!" declared Paula.

Rosita left them and went back to the sweet counter. Fanciful indeed! She'd show them. They would be eternally grateful to her. She saw herself, looking slightly aloof, surrounded by her family showering praises on her.

"Wake up, Rosie," said Toni, passing by. "Your chocolate bars are all squint."

She gave him a black look and then straightened the bars. As she lifted her head she saw Dan McGill coming into the shop. His gang was close behind him laughing and jostling and pushing one another to get in out of the rain. They shook their heads, spraying the tables with drops of water.

Toni and Paula were in the kitchen. Grandpa stood behind the counter. He straightened his shoulders when he saw the boys, ran his fingers over his moustaches.

The boys came up to the counter and leaned their elbows on it.

"Please remove your elbows," said Grandpa.

"Remove your elbows!" repeated one.

They laughed. They kept their elbows on the counter.

"We do not want your custom here," said Grandpa.

48

"What's the matter with our custom?" demanded Dan McGill.

"I do not like your money," said Grandpa.

Dan McGill laid a pound note on the counter. "Same as anyone else's. I'll have a pie and chips. Salt and vinegar."

Grandpa pushed the note back with the edge of his finger nail. "How do I know where it come from?"

"What do you mean by that, Grandpa?" Dan McGill's face tightened. Rosita held her breath. "What are you trying to say?"

"Your father gets up to no good, does he?" said Grandpa.

Dan McGill reached across the counter and seized Grandpa by the lapels of his white coat. "You stupid old fool!"

Rosita fled round to the back of the counter, calling for Toni.

Toni came quickly, looking at Dan McGill gripping his grandfather by the coat and said, "Let go of him."

Dan did not let go. "He was making remarks about my money. And my old man."

"He meant nothing by it," said Toni.

Grandpa's eyes were bulging. Paula joined them. She glared at Dan. "Bully!" she cried. Dan McGill's friends laughed.

"Tell him to apologise to me," said Dan to Toni.

"Leave go of his coat first," said Toni. "You'll hurt him. He's an old man."

"O.K., I'll leave go and he'll apologise."

"I will not apologise," said Grandpa, and brought up his right hand which held a fish slice. He whacked Dan McGill across the back of the hand. Dan yelped, withdrew his hand, and Grandpa stepped out of range. He rearranged his white coat.

"You need taught a lesson," he said.

Dan sucked his hand. His friends buzzed with anger. Toni held firmly on to the flap of the counter that separated them from their customers.

"Come on, lads," said one, surging forward. "Let's get him."

"Oh leave him alone," said Paula sharply. "He's old."

"That's the only reason I wouldn't touch him," said Dan. "If he was fifty years younger . . ."

"I will still touch you, young man," declared Grandpa. "You are a good-for-nothing!"

"For goodness sake, Grandpa!" said Paula, exasperated. "Why don't you go into the kitchen?"

"Yes," said Toni, "go into the kitchen and have a cup of coffee."

"Come on, Grandpa," said Rosita, taking his arm. He was trembling.

Dan McGill turned to his friends. "Let's blow!"

They clattered out of the café swearing loudly and knocking against chairs and tables.

Rosita led her grandfather to a chair in the kitchen and poured him some coffee from the pot on the stove. She put her arms round his neck.

"Don't be too upset, Grandpa," she said. "They're just a wild lot."

"They should show respect for their elders," he said.

"You shouldn't really have said that to Dan McGill, should you?" said Rosita gently.

"Rosita, don't tell me that you too are going to turn against me!"

Rosita sighed. She wanted to tell him that you couldn't just say what you wanted to other people, especially when you were in business. Grandpa was stubborn and there were a lot of things he didn't understand.

"It's not Dan McGill's fault if his father is in and out of prison," said Rosita.

"He looks like a hooligan," said Grandpa.

She stayed with him for a while. He drank his coffee and shook his head and muttered about the younger generation. It was all so different from when he had been a boy in Italy.

"That was a long time ago," said Rosita. "And not all boys are hooligans, Grandpa."

"Toni is all right," said Grandpa. "But the rest!"

"You think Toni's all right because you know him. Maybe if you knew some others you would like them too."

Grandpa doubted it. He muttered until his head dropped and he began to snore. Rosita kissed his rough cheek. She loved him, even though he was stubborn and sometimes silly, and only believed the things that he wanted to believe.

They did very little business the rest of the evening. Paula and Toni sat behind the counter reading, not saying much. The incident with Dan McGill had troubled them and they did not know what they were going to do about Grandpa. Their mother would have known but then she was a long way away, in Calabria. That was right down in the south of Italy, near its toe. Paula wished she were there lying in the sun, far away from the smell of chips. She had never been to Italy. Her mother had said she would take her one day, when they had the money. They always seemed to be waiting for money.

Grandpa slept in the kitchen, mouth open, hands dangling over the sides of the chair. Rosita went early to bed, though not to sleep.

When Paula came upstairs Rosita still had her light on. She put her head round Rosita's bedroom door. Rosita had a tiny room, little more than a closet, but she loved it.

"You not asleep yet?" said Paula.

Rosita, who had been sitting up in bed surrounded by sheets of thick paper, quickly began to gather them up. Her face was flushed.

"Just going to."

"What are you up to? You look kind of guilty to me."

"I am not!"

"What were you doing?" Paula tried to look at a piece of paper but Rosita snatched it away.

"I was drawing, that's all."

"O.K." Paula yawned, too tired to interest herself any further. "Good-night, kid."

As soon as Paula had gone Rosita resumed work. She continued for another hour, stopping only when she heard the church clock strike midnight. She had completed ten posters. And Susan had promised to do a few. Rosita put the posters under the bed, put out the light and closed her eyes. She thought she was going to enjoy the world of advertising.

## 6. The World of Advertising

Rosita and Susan were bursting with excitement, and spent much of the day giggling and whispering behind their hands, much to the annoyance of their teacher, Miss Bell. Rosita had a bag under her desk, a large carrier bag, the kind you get from a dress shop, full of rolled-up pieces of paper, which seemed to have something to do with the excitement. Miss Bell craned her neck a few times as she passed to try and get a better look but she could find no reason to confiscate it, and during break and lunch time Rosita removed the bag and brought it back afterwards.

After school, the two girls left the playground quickly, not dawdling around the shed as they were often inclined to do. They walked purposefully off with the large bag.

"Are you allowed to put posters up just anywhere?" asked Susan. "Are you not supposed to get a permit?"

Rosita felt scornful. Susan was much too concerned with rules and regulations and permits. Permits! You could always plead ignorance.

"I haven't the faintest idea," said Rosita. "Have you

55

got the paste? That's more important."

"It's in my bag." Susan took a pot of paste out of the plastic holdall she used for her school books. "Mum'll be wondering where all her flour's gone."

"Tell her you needed it for a project."

They were always doing projects as school and had to bring in a variety of things, old detergent boxes and pictures cut from magazines and the insides of used toilet rolls.

"So what do we do now then?" asked Susan.

"First we'll find a few suitable walls and then we'll go round the shops."

They stopped at a brick wall, the gable-end of a warehouse. There were slogans scrawled across it in chalk and paint. A few people were coming and going in the street.

"Shouldn't we wait till the coast's clear?" asked Susan.

"It never will be. We'd have to stand here all day. If we just go about our business and ignore them they'll not bother. People are funny that way."

Rosita was right. Some people did turn round to look at what they were doing but they soon passed on. No one stopped to ask if they were allowed to stick a poster on the wall.

"It's all a matter of style," said Rosita. "It's how you do things that counts."

57

"You mean it depends on how much cheek you've got," giggled Susan.

Susan held the paste pot while Rosita stuck the poster to the wall. She took her time making sure it was straight, securing each corner carefully. Then she stepped back from the wall.

"There!" she said, putting her head to one side. "It's not bad. It's bright and colourful. It should attract attention. That's what the article stressed. Impact!"

"I hope it doesn't rain. The colours'll just run."

"Susan, you're a pessimist. Anyway, even if it does, a few hundred will have seen it before it's ruined."

They went on through the streets. There were not so very many walls available when you came to examine them. Private houses were out. They put one poster on the side of a shop, Rosita doing the sticking and Susan keeping watch on the doorway for the shop-keeper. They put another on the side of a block of flats. And then they found a hoarding surrounding a building site. Wood was much easier for sticking things to than bricks or stone so Rosita was able to make a good job of this one.

"Not even a wrinkle," she said with pride.

"Do you know it's against the law to fly-post?" said a voice behind them. "You could get arrested for that."

They whirled around. Standing on the pavement in front of them was Dan McGill. Rosita glared at him. She was so taken by surprise that she could think of no squashing reply.

"What is it about then?" Dan McGill came closer to read the poster.

Rosita blocked his path. "None of your business," she said.

He laughed. "If you're sticking it up there anyone can read it."

Rosita put her back to the wall. He read the part of the poster that showed above her head.

" 'Francetti's Fish Restaurant'," he read aloud. " 'The fish restaurant with a difference . . . ' Well, well! Aren't you going to move over and let me see the rest?"

"No," declared Rosita firmly, folding her arms.

"Going to stand there all night?" He laughed again and then walked away.

"You *can't* stand there all night, Rosita," said Susan.

"Don't be silly," snapped Rosita. "Of course I'm not going to stand here all night. We're going to go and try some shops."

They did not want to go to their local ones as that would have given the game away to Toni and Paula. They had to wander quite far afield, though not too far, as people from distant areas were not likely to make the journey all the way to Francetti's Fish Restaurant from the other side of town.

Some shopkeepers were sympathetic, some quite rude. They had long chats with the sympathetic ones who listened to the tale of the Francetti's fortunes, lavishly garnished by Rosita. Susan would keep giggling and frequently had to be nudged into silence by Rosita.

"What a brave bunch of kids," said one old woman who kept a small sweet shop, "taking on hoodlums and working like slaves!"

"What else can we do?" asked Rosita modestly. "You will take a poster?"

"Surely. That'll not cost me anything."

"You are kind. If only everyone was like you!"

When they were out in the street Susan giggled again. "You fairly know how to turn on the charm, Rosita."

"What do you mean?" Rosita marched on, head in the air. Turn on the charm indeed! She was only acting naturally.

"My feet are tired," said Susan when she caught up with her. "And my throat's dry."

"Let's go and treat ourselves to a Coke." Rosita took Susan's arm. She had already forgotten Susan's remark about turning on the charm. "Come on. I'll buy you one."

They went into a café and sat by the window. It was getting dark outside and the lights were on in the shops. The Coke refreshed them. As they drank they checked on the posters they had left.

"We're doing well," said Rosita. "Only four to get rid of."

"Rosita," whispered Susan. "There's Dan McGill."

Rosita looked up. Dan McGill was sitting only a few yards away from them. He was watching them and he was grinning.

"I'm glad we amuse him so much," said Rosita and made a face in his direction, which only amused him further.

"Do you think he's following us?" asked Susan.

"Wouldn't put it past him. Probably up to no good."

"How do you mean?" Susan's eyes were round.

"Sabotage," said Rosita darkly.

"How're you doing, girls?" Dan McGill called across to them.

Rosita tossed her head. He looked so pleased with himself. Grinning like a Cheshire cat!

She rolled up the four remaining posters and put them back into the carrier bag. She picked some dried paste from her hands. The pot was almost finished and they seemed to have got paste over everything. On their hands, their clothes, the bag. Bill posting was a messy business. She stood up.

"Come on, Susan, let's go. It'll soon be too dark to see properly."

They left their table without glancing in the direction of Dan McGill. They went as far as the door and then the temptation became too much. They took a quick glance over their shoulders and there he was, still watching them, still smiling.

The next street was full of clothes shops. The girls loitered in front of a few windows looking at the clothes and shoes, choosing what they would buy if only they had the money, and if their mothers would allow them to wear the garments. They tried at one small dress shop to get their poster displayed but a thin woman in a black dress turned them away with a wave of her hand. You'd have thought they were beggars! She spoke like someone who had something large stuck in her cheek and she had a little smile of disdain round the corners of her mouth.

"Fish and chips!" she said. "Occasionally I put up an advertisement for a charity but not for a fish and chip shop."

"We need help but we're not asking for charity," said Rosita.

"If you don't mind, I'm very busy." She held the door wide open. There was no sign of a customer in the shop and when they had come in she had been learning against the wall yawning behind her scarlet-tipped fingers.

"If some people could only hear themselves!" said Rosita in a loud voice when they were back out on the pavement and before the door was closed. It shut now and the woman glared at them over the OPEN sign. "Sometimes Paula puts on a phoney voice like that, all disdainful-like. I tell her it makes her sound like a real twit."

Four other shopkeepers took the remaining posters: a greengrocer who gave them a couple of free apples apiece, a butcher, an ironmonger, and a hairdresser whose business was on the wane. Even without having read the book in the library, Rosita could see that. She promised to recommend his shop to customers in their café in return for the favour, but even as she was making the promise she wondered to whom she could sing its praises. It was the kind of hairdresser's that had a photograph of an out-of-date hairstyle in the window, one small room behind with two cracked wash-hand basins that still held the remains of other people's hair, and one elderly client with a red face reading a tattered magazine under a drier.

"Business is difficult nowadays," sighed the hairdresser, who looked no cleaner than his basins. "Competition is fierce."

Rosita agreed, and stressed the fact that she would

prefer him to put the poster in the window, and not inside the shop.

"If he puts it inside," she said to Susan once they were outside, "nobody will ever see it."

"You *are* two busy bees," said Dan McGill behind them. He was lounging against the wall with his hands in his pockets.

"Have you been following us? demanded Rosita.

"We just seem to have been going the same way."

"That'd be right!"

He straightened himself up. "You can count on me on Saturday night. I wouldn't miss it for anything. See you!" And with that, he left them.

Rosita was amazed that she had not had the last word. She always liked to. Her mother said it was a sin to be guarded against as it always made you feel you were right. Dan McGill was disturbing.

"Rosita," said Susan nervously, "I hope it's going to work out all right."

"Don't be silly! Of course it is." A slight haze of rain was falling, blurring the rooftops. The cars had put on their sidelights. People were leaving work, hurrying towards the bus stops. "I'll need to be getting home," said Rosita. "It's time for us to open up. Grandpa'll be wondering what's happened to me. But we've done a good afternoon's work, Susan. I think we've every reason to feel pleased with ourselves."

She felt full of energy as she ran homewards. She almost knocked Mr Pindi off his feet as she rounded the corner.

"Sorry, Mr Pindi," she gasped.

"I've been to visit your poor father," he told her.

"How is he?" she asked.

Mr Pindi shook his head. "Fretting about his business."

"He doesn't have to," said Rosita. "Everything's going to be all right."

She walked the rest of the way home with Mr Pindi.

"Where have you been?" fussed Grandpa, when she came in. "You usually come straight from school."

"I was out with Susan," said Rosita.

"She needs some time to see her friends," said Toni.

Rosita turned away with a little smile. If they only knew!

## 7. *Toni Makes a Discovery*

Toni sat on the upright chair beside his father's bed feeling his head sinking lower and lower without being able to do anything about it. At one point he fell asleep and only became fully awake when he almost fell off the chair. His father did not notice. He was raving about the failings of the hospital. His hands were waving freely, his leg in the pulley swinging from side to side.

"Dictatorial, my boy, that's what it is. No idea of democracy. Toni, are you listening?"

"Yes, Father."

"What's the matter with you, anyway?" Mr Francetti regarded his son suspiciously. "What have you been up to?"

"I'm just a little tired." Toni yawned and once having started, could not stop. He yawned and yawned.

"Tired? The youth of today has no stamina. When I was young . . . "

His father's voice went on. Toni yawned again and

remembered that he was supposed to read three chapters about the Russian Revolution before to-morrow morning. His history teacher had said that his injured hand might prevent him writing essays but he saw no reason why his eyes could not continue functioning.

Mr Francetti sat up and studied his son. "Everything is all right, Toni?"

"Fine."

"Your hand is mending?"

"Yes."

"Shop running well?"

"Yes, oh yes."

"Plenty of customers?"

"Yes."

"Money in the till, eh?"

"Oh indeed."

"We have little margin in our profits, Toni. We can afford no losses. So you are coping? Good. You are not a bad boy, Toni."

Just exhausted. Toni yawned once more. The takings were down and custom was falling off steadily. They would need a miracle to change their fortunes. Toni moved uneasily on his chair.

"I am glad to know all is well," said his father. "Today I heard they are insisting on sending me to a convalescent home after I leave this place. They say it would be disastrous for me to return to my shop when I am discharged from here."

"I'm sure they are right," said Toni.

"So you will manage until your Mother returns from Calabria?"

"Yes." Toni's reply was faint, but it was enough for his father.

When Toni was walking down the ward on his way out he could hear his father telling the man in the next bed what marvellous children he had been blessed with, how competent they were, how proud he was of them.

It would be three weeks until his mother returned from Italy and she might even decide to stay longer. Their grandmother was ill, she had written in her latest letter. Toni was so immersed in his thoughts that he did not see Dan McGill until he drew level with him.

"Hi," said Dan.

"Hi." Toni slowed his footsteps.

"How's Grandpa?"

"I told you before . . ." Toni sighed. "He's an old man."

"Yeah, I can see that. He ought to know better."

"I'm sorry," muttered Toni.

He and Dan had been at primary school together and been friendly, then had drifted apart when they moved up to secondary school. He thought Dan was not all that bad. It was just that he hadn't enough to do most of the time so he hung around the streets and sometimes he got into trouble.

"It's O.K.," said Dan. "I'll be coming around to your place Saturday night."

"Saturday night?"

"Sure. The big night."

"The big night?" Toni felt stupid. It must be because he was tired, he thought.

"When you're having your big bonanza of course," said Dan.

"What bonanza?" asked Toni.

"Don't tell me you don't know." Dan burst out laughing. "There are notices all over the place. There's one in a hairdresser's window in the next street."

"Notices!" Toni frowned. "I'll see you."

"Saturday!" said Dan. "I wouldn't miss it."

Toni hurried round the corner into the next street. Half-way along he found the hairdresser's. There, in the centre of the window, beside a dusty looking wig, was a large notice in glorious colours. It was reminiscent of his father's posters, the same use of colour, the same flourish, and, as he read, he realised that it had the same extravagant style. His heart dropped like a stone as he read.

'FRANCETTI'S FISH RESTAURANT:

THE FISH RESTAURANT WITH A DIFFERENCE.

Outstanding attractions on Saturday evening,
the first of many to come.
Special cut price offers on all fish and chicken suppers.
Lucky numbers for free chips.
Continuous cabaret.
Come to Francetti's, the swingingest place in town,
the place people talk of, the place people dream of,
the place you must see for yourself!
So, come to Francetti's, Saturday night!'

He opened the door of the hairdresser's. There was one man brushing a woman's hair into a high nest in front of a mirror. The shop smelt of something that reminded Toni of glue.

The hairdresser came forward, still holding the brush. He looked inquiringly at Toni.

"Can I help you? Would you like to make an appointment?"

"No thanks. It's that notice on the window. Who gave it to you?"

"Two little girls."

"I thought so." Toni sighed. "I'm sorry to trouble you, but do you think I could take it down? One of the

girls was my sister. She shouldn't have done it."

With a lot of grumbling the man retrieved the poster from the window, knocking over the wig and a tin of hair lacquer as he did so. Toni backed out of the shop apologising.

He toured the district, examining shop windows, extracting the posters he found on display, scraping some off walls with his penknife. He found it difficult and slow-going with his left hand. And at one point, when he saw a policeman coming towards him, he had to nip round the corner and hide in an alley. It would just be great if on top of everything else *he* were to be arrested for fly-posting! But he could hardly tell the constable he was taking down the posters his sister had put up. As he hid behind a dustbin, expecting a heavy hand to land on his shoulder at any moment, he wished *he* could lay a hand on *her*.

It was dark by the time he trudged back to the restaurant. The lights were on in the shop, the door was open, the juke-box playing, and there was a smell of chips. Rosita was dancing round the tables in time to the music.

"Where have you been?" Paula demanded. She had on a pink overall which she wore for frying, and her face looked hot.

Toni waved the sheaf of posters in the air, some of which were now in shreds. "Collecting posters."

Rosita stopped twirling. "You haven't taken them all down?" she cried.

"I certain have." He laid them on a table. "You've made us the laughing stock of the district."

Paula and Grandpa came to look at them. Paula started to laugh.

"I'm sorry," she said. "I can't help it."

"I'm glad you find it funny," said Toni.

"You do these, Rosita?" asked Grandpa.

"Yes," said Rosita defiantly. She glared at Toni and Toni glared at her. "Now you've spoiled everything."

"I think you have imagination, Rosita," said Grandpa. "I think you have a flair for poster writing. Just like your Father."

"Just like Father." Toni nodded. "And about as much wit!"

"What is the matter with it?" said Grandpa, spreading out his hands. "It is well-written, very nice to look at."

Toni groaned. "But look at what it says. 'Outstanding attractions. Continuous cabaret. Cut price offers.'"

"We can cut prices," said Grandpa. "That way we get more custom. The next night people come back and they pay the full price. Like in the super-markets."

"Of course we can," said Rosita. "I knew you would stand by me, Grandpa."

"The cut price bit is the least of our worries," said Toni. "It's the rest. 'The swingingest place in town!' "

Paula began to giggle. "I suppose we could make it swing."

"Sure," said Toni. "We could have you dancing on the tables."

"I had thought of that," said Rosita. "Paula's good at dancing."

*"What?"* said Paula.

" 'The place people talk of,' " read Toni grimly.

"Well, they do talk about us," said Rosita.

"But not always what we would like them to say." Toni read on. " 'The place people dream of.' Honestly, Rosita!"

"Well some people must dream about us," said Rosita.

"Nightmares. 'The place you must see for yourself.' " Toni waved his hand at the shop. "It needs redecorating and we haven't got the money."

"Susan and I are going to paint a mural on the wall," said Rosita. "We're both very fond of painting."

"That would seem obvious," said Toni, waving the posters in the air again.

"We're going to decorate the whole place, hang up Chinese lanterns, put candles in bottles." Rosita's face

74

was lit up. "And Susan's going to bring over their Christmas decorations."

"Great," said Toni.

"There's no need to be sarcastic," said Rosita. "At least we're doing something. We're trying to haul back a business from the brink of bankruptcy."

"We're more likely to be bankrupt after Saturday night."

"You've got to be bold in business, do something different from the man around the corner," said Rosita. "Sticking in the same old rut gets you nowhere."

"The child is right," said Grandpa. "By golly she is right! We need a big stir up."

"Looks like we're going to get it," said Paula.

"At the moment we're just like any other fish and chip shop," said Rosita.

"Do you think so?" said Toni.

"Toni Francetti, you have no soul." Rosita tossed her head.

Toni gave her one of his special withering looks which did not deter her.

"There's one bit that worries me particularly," he said.

"What is that?" Grandpa leaned over to have another look at a poster.

" 'Continuous cabaret.' " Toni looked at Rosita and

75

for the first time she did not look him back in the eye. "What exactly did you have in mind?"

"Well . . ."

"Well?" he demanded.

## 8. "We'll think of something"

"I agree that that is the most difficult part," Rosita admitted reluctantly.

"We do not give in when things are difficult," said Grandpa.

"You're right there," said Toni. "We even go out of our way to make things more difficult."

"I didn't have time to work out any details," said Rosita. "Susan and I have been very busy. There's a limit to what one can do."

"Thank goodness for that!"

"We thought we could sing. And play the recorder like we do at school concerts."

"This is not the same as a school concert," said Toni.

"It will probably be fifty times worse," giggled Paula.

"All you seem to be able to do is giggle." Toni turned on his sister.

"I'm sorry, I can't help it," said Paula.

"And repeat yourself," said Toni. "At least at school concerts parents come to listen to their children and think they're wonderful. No one's going to think we're wonderful!"

"I could sing too," offered Grandpa. "As a young man I had a fine voice."

No one made any comment on that, not even Rosita. They often heard him singing arias in the bath. Toni gathered up the posters and said it was time they did some work. If they were fortunate they might even have a few customers to serve.

"Don't worry, Toni," said Rosita. "We'll think of something."

"You'd better lie low," Paula advised her when Toni had gone upstairs to change his clothes.

"Toni is a very serious young man," said Grandpa. "I don't know where he gets this from."

"Mother," said Paula.

"Yes, it is not from my side of the family." Grandpa twirled his moustaches. "We were always known for our gaiety in our youth."

"Toni knows how to enjoy himself too," said Paula. "But at the moment he feels he's carrying the weight of the world on his shoulders."

"Of course. Anyway, we cannot all be the same," said Grandpa. "We need variety in this life. It is more interesting."

"You're right, Grandpa," said Rosita. "We need variety."

Variety. Rosita stood behind the counter and thought about it. She had a piece of paper and a pen in front of her. Cabaret. She wrote down the word hoping it would inspire some ideas. She would need to find some. You'd better do some fast thinking, Paula had said. The trouble was Rosita had never been to a cabaret. She had seen some things on television which she supposed would be called that. Singing and dancing, and there was often a comedian. A comedian? She had a book of jokes upstairs. But she had a feeling that Toni might not go for that.

Customers began to trickle in. As the evening progressed the numbers increased until at times the tables were full and the queue reached to the door. Grandpa sang snatches of arias under his breath as he battered fish and scooped up chips. Even Toni was smiling as he moved around clearing dishes with his good hand, keeping the queue under control, chatting to people he knew. Business was booming. Their takings would be much higher than they normally were on a Friday night.

"You see," said grandpa, "Rosita's posters are having an effect already."

"I think you're right," said Paula. "They've caught people's attention."

"But we still have tomorrow night to get through," said Toni. "Don't forget that!"

79

Towards the end of the evening Paula saw Dan McGill come in. He joined the end of the queue. When he arrived opposite her she looked up and smiled at him.

"Fish supper please," he said.

"Carry-out?"

"No. I'll have it on a plate."

She gave him the biggest piece of fish she could find and added an extra scoop of chips.

"I'm sorry about the other night," she said awkwardly. "So is Grandpa, I think, but he's too proud to say so."

"Ah, forget it!" said Dan.

He sat down in a corner. The queue diminished, the last customers came and went. Dan remained where he was.

Paula went over to him. "Fancy a cup of coffee?"

"Wouldn't mind."

She poured two cups and carried them to his table. He took some money from his pocket.

"No, have this on the house," she said.

"Thanks. Are you going to join me?"

She took off her overall and sat down.

In the kitchen Toni was stacking the dishwashing machine with his good hand. "Trust Paula!" he said. "Here we are snowed under with work and she's sitting gazing into a boy's eyes."

"She is just being nice to him," said Grandpa. "Leave her alone. She's worked hard this week. Maybe the young man needs someone to be nice to him."

"Grandpa!" said Toni. "What are you saying? The other night you smacked him over the hand with a fish slice and tonight you say he needs someone to be nice to him!"

"Well, maybe I was a bit hasty." Grandpa pottered off down to the other end of the kitchen.

Toni rolled his eyes. "Honestly! Grandfathers!"

From time to time Rosita went to the door and looked in at Paula and Dan McGill. They did not notice her. They were talking, their heads close together over the coffee cups. Rosita longed to know what they were talking about. She was far too nosey, Toni told her. It would get her into big trouble one of these days.

Eventually Dan got up to go. "See you tomorrow," he said.

"Yes," said Paula. "See you." She locked the door behind him.

"See you, lover boy," said Rosita in a high-pitched voice.

"Oh, you shut up! Honestly, kid sisters are a pain in the neck."

"Not as bad as older ones. Don't tell me I'm going

to have to put up with you trailing around looking all soppy."

"He's quite nice though, don't you think?" said Paula. "He just puts it on pretending to be tough."

"I think he's gorgeous, I must not say!" said Rosita and Paula scowled at her.

"Why don't you two go to bed?" said Toni wearily. "We've got a big day ahead of us tomorrow."

## 9. Saturday Morning

"Another bag of potatoes, Mr Abbot," said Toni.

"Expecting lots of customers tonight, Toni?" asked Mr Abbot the greengrocer.

"Maybe." Toni shrugged. He bent to pick up the potatoes, and Mr Abbot helped him carry them across the street. Blood was showing through the bandage on Toni's right hand.

"You must take care of that hand," said Mr Abbot.

"That's not so easy."

The street was busy since it was Saturday morning. Women hurried in and out of shops, children dawdled carrying large shopping bags, babies sat patiently in their prams on the pavement. Toni usually liked Saturday mornings: he liked the busyness, the air of scurry and expectancy. This morning he did not like it so much. His stomach felt queasy every time he thought of the fiasco ahead.

"O.K., Toni?" said Mr Abbot as they eased the sack of potatoes round the door of the shop. He was puffing and blowing with the effort.

"Fine, thanks."

Mr Abbot rested his hands on his plump hips and looked round with interest. Chinese lanterns hung from the ceiling, paper chains were looped from light to light, shivers of silver tinsel dangled from all the display cases.

"Christmas has come early this year," he observed.

"All we need is Santa Claus," said Toni.

"Pity it isn't Christmas," said Rosita. "Mr Abbot would have made a fine Santa Claus."

Mr Abbot laughed. His whole body shook when he laughed. He smacked his hands together.

"You're a great girl, Rosita."

Rosita rewarded him with a smile before turning back to her painting. Susan was working away at the mural, biting her lip, frowning with concentration. Her jeans and sweater were spattered with paint.

"What are you doing?" asked Mr Abbot, going to look.

"Trying to bring the Caribbean into the shop," said Rosita. "A touch of sun and warm sea and sand."

"The Caribbean?" said Toni, joining Mr Abbot.

"Why do you have to keep repeating things like an idiot?" said Rosita.

"I need to check that my ears have always heard correctly. Usually they have. Unfortunately."

"And what is the matter with the Caribbean?" Rosita added another touch of green to the water.

"I have always wanted to go there for a holiday," said Mr Abbot. "One day perhaps. When I retire."

"You should go now," said Rosita. "I don't believe in waiting."

Toni looked at the mural. It was almost finished. The girls had painted some calypso singers on the beach with palm trees behind. They were copying it from a picture in a book. It was not at all bad though Toni was not going to admit it.

"I suppose it could be worse," he said.

"Thanks a lot," said Rosita.

"I think it is brilliant, absolutely marvellous," said Mr Abbot. "I must commission you to paint a mural for me on the wall of my shop."

"Would you, Mr Abbot?" said Susan.

"Why not? I'd pay you of course."

"Oh Mr Abbot!" Rosita flung her arms round his neck and kissed his cheek. "You are a sweetie-pie."

Mr Abbot's cheeks were tinged with pink. "You Italians are all the same," he said. But he was obviously pleased.

"Not true," said Toni, but they were not listening to him. They were discussing murals, possible motifs, arranging for a day to start work. As he listened he thought Rosita might well end up with more money than either he or Paula. She was inventive and imaginative and untroubled by the craziness of her ideas.

"Next Saturday then," Rosita called after Mr Abbot as he went out.

"Next Saturday," he called back.

"We could start up in business, Susan," said Rosita. "Go round shops doing murals. Once the idea catches on you never know how far we might go."

"Don't get too carried away," said Toni.

Rosita ignored him. "If we did one mural every Saturday morning from now until Christmas how much money could we make, Susan?" she asked. Susan was better at arithmetic than she was. Susan began to count.

"I'd better see if I can get Grandpa to make a start on peeling the potatoes," said Toni. "Without them we won't even be able to open up."

"We've made up a calypso," said Rosita. "Don't you want to hear it before you go?"

"A calypso?" Toni paused. "Yes, well, maybe I'd better."

Rosita and Susan stood side by side. "Ready?" said Rosita. Susan nodded.

As they sang they swayed together, waving their brushes about, sprinkling the floor with drops of paint.

" 'Come to Francetti's for your fish,
  Come as often as you wish.
  The chips are the best to be had in town

And the Coca-Cola is never watered down.' "

"That's the first verse," said Rosita, breaking off.
"And now the chorus."

" 'Oh Francetti's, fish, fish, fish!
    Come as often as you wish.' "

"We thought everyone could join in the chorus,"
said Susan.

"What's the matter with you, Toni?" asked Rosita.
He had sat down at the nearest table.

"I just feel a bit weak round the knees, that's all."

"Do you want to hear some more?"

"Do you mean there *is* more?"

"We've got ten verses done so far."

"*Ten?*"

"Yes. Once you start you find you can go on for
ever."

Toni fled to the kitchen. Grandpa was there
preparing the fish.

"Ah Toni, my boy, I want to ask your advice. What
do you think I should sing tonight? Do you think I
should sing the aria from *Don Giovanni?* It is my
favourite opera. You know the aria, the one that goes
like this – " Grandpa burst into song.

"Grandpa, do you think it would be wise for you to
sing at all?"

"What do you mean – wise?"

"Well, the doctor did say you should take care of

your throat. You had all that trouble last winter."

"My throat is in fine order." Grandpa put back his head and tapped it with his forefinger, then he resumed his singing.

Toni returned to the café. Rosita and Susan were putting the finishing touches to the mural and singing at the same time.

" 'Fish and chips, chicken too.

Don't you know what is good for you?

Black puddings with delicious taste.

You may be sure none go to waste.

Oh Francetti's – ' "

"Hey!" yelled Toni. "Could you stop that racket for a second."

"Susan," said Rosita, "aren't you fortunate you don't have a brother?"

"I only wanted to ask you where Paula was?" said Toni. "I haven't seen her since breakfast."

"Neither have I," said Rosita. "But I think I know where she is."

"Where?" asked Toni.

"Drinking coffee in the 'Rendezvous' with Dan McGill." Rosita grinned and rolled her eyes.

"Of all the selfish little – " Toni stopped. "I'm off to the hospital. I promised I'd look in and see Father this morning."

The girls began singing again.

" 'Oh Francetti's, fish, fish, fish!

Come as often as you wish.' "

Toni walked out into the street. As he passed the haberdasher's, Mrs Small popped out of her door. "I'll be coming tonight, Toni," she called. "Is there anything I can do to help?"

No, he assured her, there was nothing. He hurried on through the streets to the hospital. He explained to the Sister that he would have to work in the shop in the afternoon and would not be able to come at the normal visiting hour. She said that under the circumstances she would make an exception and allow him to go in for ten minutes. "We have to make a lot of exceptions where your father is concerned, Toni." She smiled. "But one thing I'll say for him, he keeps the ward cheerful. Sometimes too much so, mind you. The man in the next bed burst one of his stitches yesterday he was laughing so much."

Mr Francetti was sitting up in bed eating black grapes. "Mr Abbot sent them in to me. Our neighbours are very generous. Sit down, boy, sit down." He plucked a fat grape from the stem and put it into his mouth.

Toni sat.

"I hear you're having a concert tonight," said Mr Francetti. "Mr Pindi was telling me all about it. My children tell me nothing. I have to rely on getting information from other sources."

"I didn't want to worry you," said Toni.

"Worry me? That doesn't worry me. I only wish I could be there."

A nurse passed down the ward. "Eating again, Mr Francetti." she clucked.

"Have a grape, nurse." He held out the bunch.

"Not allowed to eat on duty."

"Father, I think you get away with murder," said Toni.

"Murder, no, Toni. That would not interest me. But eating grapes is harmless. Now then, tell me all about the concert!"

Toni left a few minutes later. He took the route home that would pass by the 'Rendezvous'. As he approached he saw Paula sitting beside the window with Dan McGill. She was laughing and so was he. They looked happy. Toni walked past. He had not the heart to go in and drag her out. Looking at them had made him think of a girl in his class at school called Jane. She had straight fair hair and big green eyes and she usually smiled at him. He had often thought of asking her to go out but so far had not dared to. Next week he would ask her to have coffee with him on Saturday morning. Why not? She could only say no. But he was hopeful she would say yes. He walked the rest of the way whistling.

## 10. Saturday Night

By late afternoon Grandpa had a sore throat. He had sung so much in the course of the day that his voice would only emerge in a hoarse rasp.

"Thank goodness for that," said Toni to Paula.

"This is terrible, terrible," croaked Grandpa. "Never in my life does this happen to me. And at such a moment!"

"It might be better for your throat if you stopped talking," suggested Paula. "Rest it."

"Rest it? I must recover it." Grandpa hurried along the street to the chemist's to buy throat lozenges. He sucked one every ten minutes and wound a thick scarf around his throat.

"If you go on sucking those things you'll end up being sick," said Paula.

"I am prepared for that as long as I can sing," said Grandpa.

"And we are prepared for anything as long as he doesn't sing," said Paula when he had moved out of earshot.

"Paula, have you stopped to think what we *are*

going to do this evening?" said Toni. "People are going to be coming here expecting to be entertained."

"Perhaps they will be," said Paula with one of her mysterious looks.

"Calypsos from Rosita and Susan? You must be joking. We'll be the laughing stock of the district. Listen to them now."

They stood in the doorway of the kitchen and looked into the café. Rosita and Susan were weaving their way in and out of the tables singing yet another verse of their endless calypso.

" 'Chips with vinegar, chips with sauce,

Lovely creamy batter in which the fish can toss.

Everything you want you will find it here,

From white pudding suppers to good cheer.

Oh Francetti's – ' "

There were a few children in buying chips to take home for tea. At the end of the chorus Rosita cried, "Come on then, join in the chorus. Ready?"

" 'Oh Francetti's fish, fish, fish!

Come as often as you wish.' "

The children joined in. A few hesitated at first and giggled but gradually they were sucked in by Rosita's enthusiasm.

"Rosita could get blood out of a stone," observed Paula.

"Kids maybe," said Toni. "But what about later when

we get the older ones in? The likes of Dan McGill."

"There's nothing wrong with Dan McGill." Paula rounded on him sharply.

"But his friends."

"Some of them are all right."

"And some of them aren't."

"We'll deal with those," said Paula.

"You sound very confident. Have you something up your sleeve?"

Paula smiled. "I must go and prepare the chickens."

A crowd of men came in. They were noisy but in a good mood. They wore football club scarves. Their team had won. They occupied all the tables and after the two girls had sung a verse of their calypso the men joined in with gusto and then encouraged the girls to continue. "More, more!" they shouted and Rosita and Susan were only too happy to oblige.

" 'When your team has won, what more could you
    wish,
  Than a lovely piece of juicy fresh fish,
  Served with chips that are golden brown,
  And a pot of tea to wash it all down?' "

The men cheered and joined in the chorus.

" 'Oh Francetti's, fish, fish, fish . . . ' "

"They enjoy themselves, yes?" said Grandpa, as he stood behind the counter watching the scene. "Rosita has talent. She takes after me."

He was still croaking, Toni noted thankfully, and even if he did insist on singing they could put a record on in the juke-box at the same time to drown him out.

Before the football men left they showered the tables with coins for Rosita and Susan. The girls scooped them up joyfully.

"I'm not sure if you should be taking money for singing," said Toni. "We haven't got an entertainment licence. You'll be singing in cinema queues next and getting moved on by the police." But in spite of what he said Rosita could see that he was not annoyed. It was just his way: he liked to get his grumble in and then he felt better.

"I wonder if I would like to be a cabaret singer when I grow up," mused Rosita.

"A few hours ago you were going to be an artist specialising in murals," said Toni.

"There are a lot of things I would like to be. Oh Toni, isn't it marvellous when you think of all the things you could do!" She twirled around. Her eyes shone. Toni put out his hand and ruffled her hair.

"You're a daft thing," he said. "Go on, there's someone at your counter, go and serve them."

"O.K. My throat could do with a rest anyway."

"I'm sure it could. Professional singers have to take care of their throats, so I'm told."

She made a face at him before she went to the counter.

The queue for the chip counter reached the door. Toni put some money into the juke-box.

"Don't tell me that's the cabaret," said one youth.

"No," said Toni, "we're taking a break."

Cabaret! He cursed Rosita under his breath. That girl and her use of words, her delight in anything flamboyant. He joined his grandfather and Paula behind the counter. They were working without pausing and the old man had no time even to test his voice. Toni did what he could with his good hand.

"Don't worry," said Paula. "Help is on its way."

She glanced at the door from time to time. So too did Toni, but all he saw were more and more customers crowding in to take advantage of the cheap offers. That might be enough for them: the thought of saving a few pence, without bothering about the entertainment part.

And then three of Dan McGill's gang arrived.

"We've come to see what's doing," said one. He looked round. "Not much by the looks of it!"

"Susan and I could do some verses of our calypso," said Rosita to Toni.

"Don't tell me you sing calypsos?" said the boy. To his friends he said, "Hey, what about that?"

"Not just now, Rosita," said Toni quickly. "Later

maybe." He knew the boys would laugh at Rosita and Susan. They would laugh at almost anybody.

"Come on, Susan," cried Rosita, "let's sing!"

" 'Crispy spring rolls, curried or plain,

They will make you want to come again,

Or if you prefer a tender chicken breast,

Just put in your order and we'll do the rest.' "

"All together now," shouted Rosita and went into the chorus.

" 'Oh Francetti's fish, fish, fish!

Come as often as you wish.' "

"One more time!" Rosita waved her hand like the music teacher did when she was conducting the school choir.

Most people joined in the chorus the second time round and at the end of it there was a great stamping of feet and clapping of hands and someone shouted "Bravo!" And if the three members of Dan McGill's gang laughed, then they were not heard in the general commotion.

"Ready with another verse, Susan? Let's do the one about the white puddings and haggis."

But before they could begin Paula said, "Hang on! Here comes Dan."

Rosita could not see why the arrival of Dan McGill should stop them singing. Now that she had got into the swing of it she felt that she really could have kept going all evening. It was amazing how new verses just kept popping into her head.

Dan came pushing his way through the crowd carrying a guitar. He was followed by two of his friends, one of whom also carried a guitar and the other a drum. The three who had come in earlier were looking at one another with raised eyebrows.

"Hey, Mick!" Dan called to one of them. "I've been looking all over for you. Coming to sing with us?"

"Well," said Mick, hesitating.

"Ah, come on," said Dan.

"Help them through, Toni," said Paula. She was smiling.

With a family like his, Toni could no longer be surprised at anything. He shouted, "Make way there and let the boys through."

"I thought we'd shove two tables together," said Paula, "and let them sit on top."

"But that means less sitting space," objected Toni.

"People will just have to stand tonight."

"I suppose you're right," said Toni.

The tables were put together, the four boys climbed up. Dan winked at Paula and she smiled back at him.

"Paula has her uses at times," said Rosita to Susan. In spite of not being able to go on with her calypso at the moment, she thought some music was a good idea.

The boys began to play and the café came suddenly

alive. Paula and Grandpa scooped up the chips more quickly, Rosita and Susan ran to and fro between the shop and the kitchen bringing fresh batches of potatoes and fish. Soon the shop was packed until it was scarcely possible to squeeze anyone else in. Toni had to move some people out who had been in for a long time. The queue stretched right along the pavement.

When Rosita saw Mandy and her two friends peering round the door she waved. They scuttled off and Rosita smiled. So much for five pound notes and recording studios! They could go and sit in the 'Sea Breezes'. From the looks of things, they would be the only customers the place would have.

Mrs Small, Mr Pindi and Mr Abbot were given special seats by the wall where they would not be jostled. Mrs Small had brought her knitting. Mr Pindi sat very upright, smiling, after he had eaten his spring roll and chips. Mr Abbot kept saying, "It just shows what you can do with a bit of initiative. That girl's got talent right enough."

Toni went out to take a look at the queue and try to estimate if they could cope with all the waiting customers. They'd need to work like mad, peeling and frying and serving. As he was about to go back inside he caught sight of a familiar figure coming long the street carrying a suitcase. He stared. It couldn't be! Yes, it was – it was their mother!

He ran to meet her.

"Mother, what on earth are you doing here?" he said.

"What a way to greet me!" She put down her case.

"Did Father cable you?"

"No. What has happened to your father?" demanded Mrs Francetti. "Come on, tell me! I can sense it."

"He fell off the roof and broke his leg," said Toni.

His mother tossed back her hair. "I might have known it. The minute I turn my back he does something stupid. That is why I have returned."

"But you were supposed to stay away at least a month."

"Well, I stayed for two weeks," she said. "That was enough. I saw your grandparents and they saw me. We spoke to one another and then we had nothing further to say. Your grandmother had a bad cold but she recovered. We all sat in the sun and they slept and so I thought to myself, 'What am I doing sitting here in the sun in Calabria beside my sleeping aged parents when I could be back with my family where I belong seeing that they get into no troubles?' "

"Yes, well . . . " Toni looked back towards the shop. The queue had stretched even farther, the music had grown louder. Dan McGill might not be the best musician the town had to offer but what he lacked in expertise he made up for with enthusiasm.

"What is that noise?" asked his mother suspiciously.

"It's a group."

"A group? A pop group?"

"Yes," said Toni. "Playing and singing."

"In the *shop*?" said Mrs Francetti.

Toni nodded.

"We do not run a disco!" Mrs Francetti went purposefully forward. Toni picked up her suitcase and followed. The doorway was blocked.

"I cannot even get into my own restaurant." She put her hands on her hips.

"But we're making a fortune, Mother."

"That may be but I would still like to get inside."

Toni cleared a path for her. When she reached the counter Grandpa dropped a fish supper on the floor and cried, "Maria, what are you doing here?"

"Mother!" yelled Rosita, jumping on top of her and almost strangling her.

"Now don't fuss, Mother," said Paula after she had kissed her. "Why don't you go upstairs and lie down? You must be tired after your journey."

"Don't fuss, says my daughter." Mrs Francetti examined Paula. "What has happened to my daughter in my absence? I've only been gone two weeks. Long enough by the looks of it! As for lying down, I am not in the least bit tired. Quite the contrary. I have not felt so full of energy for two weeks."

She took off her coat and went at once behind the counter. "Next please," she called.

They closed the doors at midnight.

"The till is bulging," cried Grandpa. "We are rich!"

"Don't exaggerate, Grandpa," said Mrs Francetti. "But we have certainly taken more than we usually do on a Saturday night."

"We have taken more tonight than we take in a week," said Toni, who was starting to count. "Father will be pleased. We ought to pay you something, Dan," he added, looking up.

"Oh no, we don't want anything," said Dan.

Paula was feeding him and his friends with large pieces of chicken and enormous helpings of chips. Mrs Francetti sat down to eat too. She had not eaten for hours.

"It's nice to be back," she said, looking round. "Troublesome as you are, I have missed you all."

"And we have missed you, Maria," declared Grandpa.

"I daresay," said Mrs Francetti. "In some ways. In others I expect you have been quite pleased to have me out of the way. Don't bother to deny it! Susan, shouldn't you be away home to your bed?"

"Her mother said she could stay the night," said Rosita.

Rosita and Susan began to sing again. Dan picked up his guitar and strummed, accompanying them.

" 'Come to Francetti's for your fish,
　　Come as often as you wish.
　　The chips are the best to be had in town
　　And the Coca-Cola is never watered down.' "

"Now the chorus, everyone," cried Rosita, and they all joined in, even their mother.

" 'Oh Francetti's fish, fish, fish!
　　Come as often as you wish.' "

"Let's have a party," said Paula.

"Yes, let's!" said Toni.

They looked at their mother.

"You might as well," said Mrs Francetti. "It'll be back to normal tomorrow. Frying as usual."

*Some other Puffins by Joan Lingard*

## THE FREEDOM MACHINE

Mungo dislikes Aunt Janet, and to avoid staying with her he decides to hit the open road and look after himself, and with his bike he heads northwards bound for adventure and freedom. But he soon discovers that freedom isn't quite what he'd expected, especially when his food supplies are stolen, and in the course of his journey he learns a few things about himself.

## GLAD RAGS

Sam and Seb can't wait to join their parents Torquil and Isabella in the Greek Islands. Even Granny is excited – so excited that her hair turns orange! But nothing in this family ever seems to go to plan and the eagerly awaited Greek holiday is no exception.

The holiday isn't the only problem. There's Seb falling in and out of love with Viola, Torquil falling in and out of a job, and the whole family falling in with a plan to save a damp old castle!

## RAGS AND RICHES

When Sam and Seb's mother, Isabella, discovers a coat lined with a thousand pounds in her own second-hand clothes shop, she doesn't know what to do with it. But money isn't their only problem. There's Granny who falls in and out of love with a butcher and there's the saga of Seb and his heart-throb Viola. Will he ever ask her out?